Clara's Journey

By Dr. Cynthia F. Jones, Ed.D

Illustrations by Genevieve Zzyzyx

This story is a work of historical fiction imagined and based on published facts about the life and accomplishments of Clara Brown who lived from 1800 to 1885.

Dedicated to…..

Glenn for unwavering support…….

Paul who is defining his own amazing journey…

A long time ago, Clara Brown went on a journey.

This was a VERY dangerous trip – but she knew in her heart she had to go. Why go on an uncertain and scary journey to an unknown place?

Clara wanted a better life. She'd heard many amazing stories about people going west to Colorado and finding a fresh new start. Most importantly for Clara was her desire to leave the American south. Clara had been a slave all her life – now she was free and wanted a better life.

A big decision was made! Clara would find a way to reach the gold fields of Colorado. She had faith in herself that she could find work when she reached her destination. Clara had always worked hard, cleaning clothes and cooking meals, and now she planned to use her skills as a free woman out west.

Now that she had decided to begin her journey, a huge challenge stood in Clara's way. How would she get to Colorado from Missouri? No one would sell ex-slaves train or stagecoach tickets because slavery had not yet been abolished. So even though Clara had a small amount of money, left to her by her owner when he died, she could not buy a ticket to travel.

And then amazing good luck came her way! Clara learned that a wagon train going west to the gold fields of Colorado needed a cook. An ex-army colonel was planning to lead a wagon train, taking gold seekers west to the Rocky Mountains.

Clara was so excited! She went to see the colonel and convinced him that she would be a valuable addition to the group by cooking the meals on the trail. Her tasty meals had always been a hit, and after sampling Clara's cooking the colonel agreed! Clara would travel west with the wagon train as cook.

So very soon the group of 26 men, with the colonel as wagon train leader, began their journey west. At last Clara was on her way to Colorado.

Miles and miles of amazing country unfolded before Clara on this eight-week journey to Colorado. Until now, she had been used to seeing only the green farm fields in the south where she had lived her life as a slave.

Clara was astonished at the flat landscapes that seemed to go on forever. Mostly the land was covered with short golden grasses, but sometimes there were small bushes or trees. Most of the traveling days offered endless skies of brilliant blue.

Occasionally there were days when storm clouds drifted across the huge open skies. On those days, thick blankets of dark gray clouds completely covered the sky, and everyone knew they should prepare for a fierce storm.

When storms hit, there was booming thunder! Gigantic lightning bolts would streak through the sky toward the ground! Storms also brought buckets and buckets of rain! The sound and feel of the thunder, so loud and strong, rattled Clara's teeth.

Storm days made travel so much harder than normal. Muddy puddles formed quickly on the trail, but Clara didn't mind one bit – her spirits were high! She had confidence that she was going toward a better life.

At the end of each day, when the wagon train stopped to camp for the night, Clara's work began. As cook for the entire group, Clara got busy preparing a huge and hearty meal for dinner. It was also her job to be up before sunrise and prepare an early breakfast, because the wagon train had to get back on the trail and keep making progress to Colorado. Clara was so grateful that her skills as a cook had given her this opportunity.

The plan to go west had been a major decision for Clara, and a VERY risky and unusual journey for a black woman traveling alone in 1859.

But Clara had good reasons to make this risky journey. The American south, where Clara had spent her entire life, was a very unfriendly place to be as an ex-slave. Clara was one of the lucky ones. She had her freedom now because her owner had wished it to be so after he died. This kind-hearted good man also left her a small amount of money. When he died, his wife honored his wishes and said a tearful farewell to Clara.

Another reason that Clara was willing to take this journey was that the southern part of America was very, very dangerous for freed slaves. Men or women who had gained their freedom were sometimes captured and sold back into slavery by cruel and greedy slave traders – ex-slaves had virtually no protection from the law.

So even though the decision to become a pioneer headed for the western frontier was dangerous and daring, Clara was eager to take the chance. She wanted to escape the hostile places of her past.

During the long days walking west with the wagon train, Clara's thoughts constantly went back to memories of the family she'd lost during her time as a slave. Her husband, she'd learned, had died after being sold to a new owner far away from the plantation where Clara had lived. Sadly, three of her four children had also been sold away from her. Clara's fourth child had died in an accident while she was a very young girl. So as far as Clara knew, she had three living children somewhere in the south. Her secret hope and prayer were that she would find a way to locate them someday.

Every single day the secret sorrow of her precious lost family made Clara's heart ache. But she would not let these painful memories hold her back.

After several weeks and many miles of slow and steady traveling west, Clara began to see gradual changes on the horizon. The Rocky Mountains of Colorado were becoming visibly larger – what a magnificent sight!

That evening, as the group settled in and gathered around the campfire for their meal, the colonel announced that they would finally reach Denver, Colorado in about three days.

Clara was super excited and just a bit nervous all at the same time! She was almost there! The journey had been a long and hard trail to conquer, but it would soon be over.

The wagon train had been lucky to be almost at the end of their journey with no major problems. Fierce storms, muddy trails, and thick clouds of stinging flies and mosquitoes had challenged the travelers almost daily, but for pioneers going west, these things were to be expected.

The biggest danger on this journey had been the possibility of attacks by Native American tribes who did not like west bound travelers crossing and invading their lands – and who could blame them? Clara's wagon train had been lucky; many other pioneer groups had not been so fortunate. Many other wagon train travelers had encountered tragedy and death as native warriors attacked.

Finally, after a few more days of travel, as the horses worked hard pulling the wagons up the steep and winding road to the foothills of the Rocky Mountains, Clara reached Denver, Colorado. When the wagon train reached town, everyone went their separate ways to begin their new lives in the west.

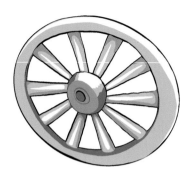

Several Years Later

Central City, Colorado

Clara was now settled in comfortably as a resident of Central City, Colorado.

During her short time in Denver, when the wagon train trip had ended several years ago, Clara learned that Central City, a growing new mining town, was just two days travel up the mountain. From all Clara learned about this new and booming town, she felt that was where she needed to be.

When Clara had arrived years ago, Central City, which was then named Gregory Gulch, was barely a town. There were rows and rows of tents creating a ragged and unorganized little settlement. But oh my – it was bustling with life and excitement! Central City was growing into a real town with the daily arrival of miners who hoped to strike it rich finding gold in the mountains.

Settling in Central City turned out to be a smart move for Clara. As the years passed, the ragged little tent city grew into a prosperous mountain mining town. Rich veins of gold were found in the hills above and around Central City.

The promise of gold meant that the would-be miners needed supplies and services, so Central City grew to serve their needs. Sticking to what she knew how to do – and using the small sum of money she'd received when she was freed from slavery – Clara opened a laundry business.

It didn't take long for word to spread about the amazing job that Clara did with laundry that customers left with her. Her best customers were miners coming into town from their mine claims to resupply themselves before heading back to work in the hills.

Then Clara recognized another opportunity because these men needed meals. As an excellent cook, she added a tent next to her laundry as an eating establishment (she had hired a partner to help her in the laundry).

"Aunt Clara's," as her restaurant became known, was wildly popular as a place for hearty, tasty meals, and her businesses continued to grow.

Central City was now a recognized, prosperous town and firmly on the map! As the town grew and Clara saved the money she earned from her laundry and restaurant businesses, she was able to have a lovely house built. Clara made this house as large as she could, with many extra rooms, because she secretly hoped that one day she might find members of her missing family, and they would always have a place to stay with her.

But for now, since she was still alone, Clara began to offer lodging to a few unfortunate souls who needed a place to stay. Without intending to make this happen, Clara was now in the boarding house business. And Clara never turned away a hungry or needy person who might be down on his luck and in need of help.

Her home even served as a small hospital for a few injured miners. Some of the men who came down from the hills were so worn down that they needed care and rest in order to get back to work in the mines, or to head home as some of them did if they had not been successful in finding gold in the hills. Clara became known as the Angel of the Rockies.

As a result of Clara meeting a variety of miners who needed care, she befriended one grizzly old gold prospector who wanted to keep working his mine but had run out of money. An idea occurred to the busy mind that Clara always kept working. She was always looking toward the future.

The old miner needed money and Clara's growing fortune was enough for her to begin additional business investing. So as a result, Clara purchased part interest in this prospector's gold mine. Now she was in the business of gold mines!

As time went on, Clara acquired several additional mining claims. Some were outright given to her for her generosity in helping broken-down miners; others she purchased with her growing wealth.

Clara had never dreamed that she would become prosperous. But by the standard of the time she lived in, Clara was now a wealthy woman.

With her growing fortune, Clara felt strongly that it was important to be an active and contributing part of the community in which she lived. She became known as a generous donor and philanthropist to causes that helped people in need.

The founding of the first non-denominational church in Central City was established in part by large contributions from Clara. Through her work with the church missionaries, a fine church came into existence. The establishment of this church was a true sign of the growth of Central City into a real town, as black and white citizens of the town worshiped together.

By all outward measures, Clara Brown was a huge success as a pioneer. She'd come west, and against all odds made a place for herself in the newly emerging west of America. However, her lost family was never far from her mind.

Now that Clara could read and write – she'd learned in classes offered to the community by the church missionaries – Clara began to devote a great deal of her time sending letters asking for any leads about her missing family members to as many places as possible. Never giving up hope, Clara kept up her campaign of searching through letter writing, to find out whatever she could about her three long-lost children.

After several years of getting leads that led nowhere, Clara began to put together a different plan. Part of the problem was that records of slave births, deaths, and sales were not always complete or accurate. Many of the people who might have been able to give Clara information had also been slaves, and they could not read or write because it was against the law for slaves to be educated. There were many dead ends to her extensive searches.

With renewed determination, Clara decided to do something she never thought she would do – return to the south to continue her search in person.

Traveling across the country was now much easier for ex-slaves than it was when Clara first traveled to Colorado. The Civil War was over. Slavery had been abolished, so Clara began to plan. She was determined to use her money and the rest of her life to find the answers she needed. She wanted peace of mind.

Clara began to sell some of her property, in order to pay for the searching she planned to do for her lost family by traveling back to the south.

1 Year Later

Clara had been searching and traveling for several months though the states of Missouri, Ohio, and Kentucky. Everywhere she went, she began by going to black churches in the community and asking for information about her missing family. The church community was the best source of information that simply could not be found in written records. After several months of searching and traveling, and asking questions of everyone she could, Clara still had not found any solid leads to her beloved children.

There was, however, some joy to be found. Much to Clara's surprise, she found relatives she never expected to see again and some that she'd never met. There were distant cousins, nephews, and nieces. This was a sweet and happy time for Clara after her long searches without success. Clara rejoiced in these unexpected reunions.

During Clara's travels to many locations during her search, many freed slaves hinted to her that they too would like to leave the south and start fresh in a new place – they simply didn't know how to do it.

So once again Clara's generous spirit came forward and she decided to help as many people as she could manage.

Since there was a large group of potential travelers, at least 50 people consisting of individuals and families, she had to think about the best way to get her group across the country and to her home in Colorado.

Although freed slaves could now purchase tickets to travel on trains, Clara's group was much too large to travel by train. So once again Clara found herself preparing to cross the country by wagon train – except this time she was the leader of the group!

Over the years, thousands of want-to-be settlers had traveled from the southern and eastern part of America over the prairies of the mid-west to find new futures. So as a result, the trails were much better than they were at the time of Clara's first journey west. There were also small towns where supplies could be purchased. And this was very, very fortunate because it didn't take long for Clara's group to discover, once they began the trip, that she had been badly cheated by the man who sold her the wagons and supplies. The wagon wheels were in terrible shape and began to break! A large portion of the food supplies were rotten!

However, this band of travelers would not be discouraged by any of the challenges that they faced. There were small settlements along the trail where Clara could purchase what they needed, to replace parts for the wagons and re-supply the necessary food.

The travelers led by Clara were joyful and hopeful free men and women. They had faith that they were traveling to a better life. Throughout the long eight weeks it took to reach Denver, Colorado, the group was mostly in high spirits even with the difficulties. Everyone trusted Clara's experience, wisdom, and her deep and genuine concern for every individual who was brave enough to make this journey with her.

Upon reaching Denver, some of the travelers decided to find their own way. However, others continued the short journey to Central City with Clara, and she helped everyone get settled and find a way to make a living, in order to establish themselves as free citizens of Colorado.

The Final Journey

Over the years, Clara made several trips back to the south – she would never give up looking for her lost children. Each time she returned to Colorado from her searches for family, Clara would help small groups of ex-slaves, awed by Clara's accomplishments, to return with her. Clara was much older now and wagon travel was much too hard for her, so her returning groups were very small and she would purchase train tickets for their travel.

One day, when Clara arrived home after her latest trip, there was a letter waiting for her. It was a miracle! After many years of futile searching, there was absolute confirmation that one of her daughters, Liza, was living in Iowa.

Clara lost no time! Even though she had just returned, she immediately made travel plans to reach Iowa as soon as possible!

It's hard to imagine the reunion between mother and daughter, who had not seen each other for decades. There was great joy and gratitude for Clara and Liza, who had endured so much and been separated since Liza was a young child. They were so very thankful to have found each other.

Liza went to visit her mother in Colorado several times during the remainder of Clara's life, because Clara was now elderly and her health was too fragile for any additional long and difficult travel, even by train.

Epilogue

Although Clara's greatest wish was granted when she found her daughter, it seems that fate had not yet finished with her. What was then called the storm of the century viciously hit Colorado late one spring. The storm brought flooding so severe that it's hard to imagine. The flood washed away most of Central City – as well as Clara's home and property.

When the town began to put itself back together, dishonest and greedy men boldly cheated Clara out of what had been hers by refusing to honor her claims to her property. Everyone knew what had belonged to Clara but there was nothing she could do to prove her ownership, since nearly all paper records had been washed away in the flooding.

Many people in the town churches and in the general community knew her quite well and remembered her generous spirit and service to all in need. People came together and built a small house for Clara. The community helped her financially so that she could live a comfortable but modest life until the end of her days.

Clara lived a peaceful and comfortable life in her senior years. She was content and grateful for everything because she had been successful in reuniting with one of her children.

Photo provided by Denver
Public Library Special
Collections, Z-275
with full permissions for
publication use

Born 1800 in Missouri.

At age 59 traveled by wagon train from Missouri to Colorado.

April 1865 the Civil War ended and Clara could travel freely. She liquidated her investments and began the first of many trips to the south to search for her children.

Reunited with daughter Eliza Jane in 1882.

In 1885, the last year of Clara's life- she was voted into the Society of Colorado Pioneers for her role in Colorado's early history.

Acknowledging with deep appreciation

Donna and Mr. E   for eagle eye editing, wisdom & perspective……

Genevieve illustrator extraordinaire…….

About the author Dr. Cynthia F Jones, Ed.D

This book was inspired by a visit, over 20 years ago, to the Black American West & Heritage Museum known at the time as the Black Cowboy Museum in Denver Colorado. Their display about Clara Brown captivated my interest, admiration and intention to do something to honor her legacy.

*San Diego native now living in Mesa, Arizona * Find great joy visiting art museums & creating art at home * Regularly indulge a passion for making candles & silk painting * Dedicated to teaching yoga & Nia (a dance practice) and focusing on healthy lifestyle practices in order to be fully present to the beauty in the world * Retired after 40 plus years as a university administrator & faculty member at University of Connecticut, Coe College in Iowa, and San Diego State University *

This book is available in hardback directly from the author at senoj99@gmail.com or at Amazon.com

The illustrator

Genevieve Zzyzyx lives in San Diego with her husband James, daughter Cassia, and a dusty three-legged orange tabby cat named Zamunda. Her favorite food is noodles. Her favorite vegetable is broccoli, she even painted a broccoli floret fighting a mechanical pig. She has artwork in houses all over the world from drawing souvenir cartoons for kids at the San Diego Zoo for 12 years. She learned to draw by practicing, and by listening to all her teachers' thoughtful advice. She has always been a nerd, and still likes to draw anatomical diagrams for fun, so she also works as a Medical Illustrator. Genevieve drove an ambulance to Yosemite with friends and camped on the rooftop. She curated an art gallery in South Park. She illustrated spider monkeys in the cloud forests of Nicaragua. She drew the llamas of Machu Picchu (while dizzy with altitude sickness). When she is not painting caticorns or drawing horses, she enjoys playing piano, singing, and digging in the family garden (which is mostly kale). Her mom is a soap-maker and grocery clerk. Her dad installs solar panels on rooftops in Hawaii. She loves riding her electric bicycle to the library. If she could have a magical superpower, it would be telepathy. If she could be any animal, it would be an owl because they get to sleep all day. Contact Genevieve at ColoringBookFactory@gmail.com